THE SONG OF SIX BIRDS

For my grandchildren,
a reminder of the beauty of birdsong
—R.D.

To Margaret, who loves birds
—L.G.

THE SONG OF
SIX BIRDS

BY **RENE DEETLEFS**

ILLUSTRATED BY **LYN GILBERT**

DUTTON CHILDREN'S BOOKS
NEW YORK

Lindiwe lay on her grass mat, sleepily aware of the
music of morning as it stole into her ears: cattle
lowed, buckets clanked, goats bleated.

Lindiwe yawned, then blinked her eyes. Next to her,
on the smooth, cool floor, lay an African flute, just
like the ones in the wayside store!

"Mama," she whispered, "is this flute for me?"
"Yes, Lindiwe," said her mother with a smile as she
played with the baby. "It is for you, child who loves music."

Up jumped Lindiwe.
"Mama!" she cried. "A flute is *full* of music!
Just listen!"

Putting her lips to the flute, she drew a mighty breath and blew. What a shattering noise! The dozing dog started up and howled. The chickens squawked, and the baby screamed with fright.

Lindiwe peered into the dark tunnel of her
flute. There was no sign of music there.
　What's wrong with this flute? Lindiwe wondered.
I must find music for it.

So off she went—past two old mamas weaving grass mats,
all the way to the river in search of music for her flute.

"Mahem!" called a crowned crane, preening himself in the morning sunlight.

"Crane," begged Lindiwe, "share your trumpet call with me! This flute needs music."

"Mahem!" trumpeted the royal bird.
The echo of his call flew into Lindiwe's flute.
"Thank you!" she shouted, jumping from stone
to stone as she crossed the river.

A boy was herding goats on the other side.
"Tock-tocki-tock," a hornbill called from a rock.
"Hornbill," said Lindiwe, "you see my flute? It
is new and cannot yet sing like you. Share with
me a 'tocki-tock.'"

The hornbill obliged, and into Lindiwe's
flute fell the bright, round sound.
"Thank you, Hornbill!" she cried.

Along a dusty path, a woman was hanging blankets on a bush to air. Unseen, a bird sang, "Doo, doo-doo-doo."

Quiet as a mouse, Lindiwe listened to the soft, falling notes.

"Don't hide from me, Rainbird," she whispered.
"This flute needs a song from you."
But the rainbird would not open its beak.

So Lindiwe waited, and waited. . . .
At last, from among the leaves, the rainbird appeared. Holding out her flute, Lindiwe quickly caught a "Doo-doo-doo."
"Thank you, shy Rainbird," she said softly.

Then suddenly Lindiwe shrieked.
A hornet's sting had burned her arm.

Off she ran to the village medicine man, who was
quietly gathering herbs nearby.
"Look at my arm!" sobbed Lindiwe. "And my poor
flute! I don't want the sound of sobs inside it!"

The wise old man smiled, laying a
cool herb leaf on her throbbing arm.
   "But a flute should sometimes sob,"
he said. "Ask that hoopoe."

Lindiwe turned and saw the hoopoe, searching the ground for insects. Raising and lowering his crest he called, "Hoop, hoop," the notes catching in his throat like the sound of quiet crying.

Lindiwe wiped away her tears. "Hoopoe, please share your song with me."

"Hoop, hoop!" he called again. Lindiwe smiled.
The mellow song was safely in her flute.

On the edge of the village, Lindiwe stood aside for an old man riding his bicycle. A jar, heavy with honey, was balanced on his carrier. Following him was a Paradise flycatcher.

"Whee-wheeo-wit-wit!" The tiny ripple of sound settled on the tip of Lindiwe's flute.

Wheewheeo wit-wit--

Now the sun hung low and Lindiwe's shadow was long. Just before the sun set, a wood owl called: "Whoo-hu, whoo-hu-hu!"

Lindiwe caught the sound in her flute. She
peered into it, and a smile spread slowly over
her face. The song of six birds filled it.

Lindiwe hurried home, followed
by the six birds. They all made
music while she ran.

Their joyous sounds carried through the village, calling everyone to join in the fun.

Humming and swaying to the music,
the two old mamas left their looms. Then the boy
and his goats came capering along. The woman with
the blankets whistled and skipped. Prancing and chanting
came the medicine man, and then—dancing like he used
to long ago—came the old man with the bicycle. Lindiwe's
mother, hearing all the jolly sounds, smiled proudly.

"Here, my child of music," she said, "I have made my special stew so all can join in a feast."

Now eating, now singing, now dancing, the happy party lasted long into the night. The air was filled with the music of Lindiwe's flute—and the song of six birds.

Library of Congress Cataloging-in-Publication Data
Deetlefs, Rene.
The song of six birds/ by Rene Deetlefs;
illustrated by Lyn Gilbert.—1st ed.   p. cm.
Summary: Wishing to make beautiful music,
Lindiwe captures the songs of six birds in her new flute.
ISBN 0-525-46314-3 (hardcover)
[1. Flute—Fiction. 2. Music—Fiction. 3. Birds—Fiction.
4. Blacks—Africa—Fiction. 5. Africa—Fiction.] I. Gilbert, Lynn, ill. II. Title.
PZ7.D3596So   2000   [E]—dc21   99-25587   CIP

Published in the United States 2000 by Dutton Children's Books,
a division of Penguin Putnam Books for Young Readers,
345 Hudson Street, New York, New York 10014
http://www.penguinputnam.com/yreaders/index.htm

Originally published in Great Britain 1999 by Andersen Press Ltd., London
Typography by Alan Carr • Printed in Italy
First American Edition
2 4 6 8 10 9 7 5 3 1